My First Book

Colin and Jacqui Hawkins

Viking Kestrel

My first day home

My first smile

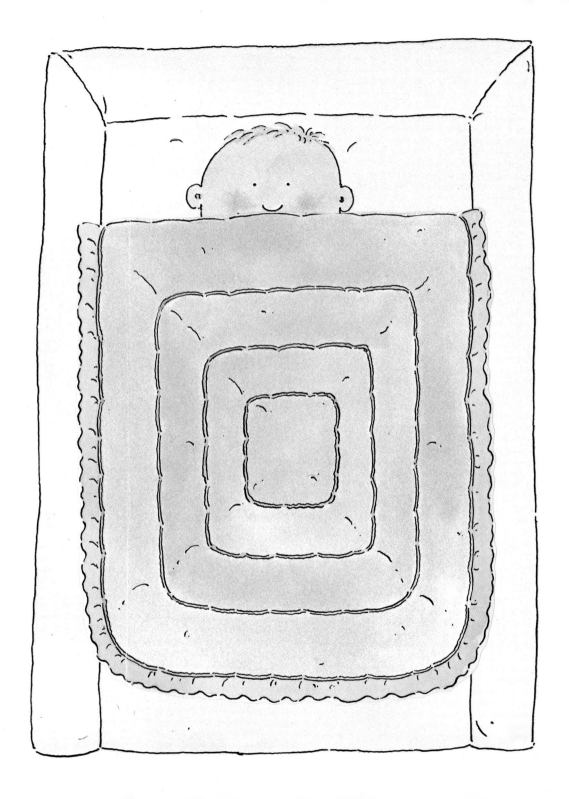

My first day sitting up

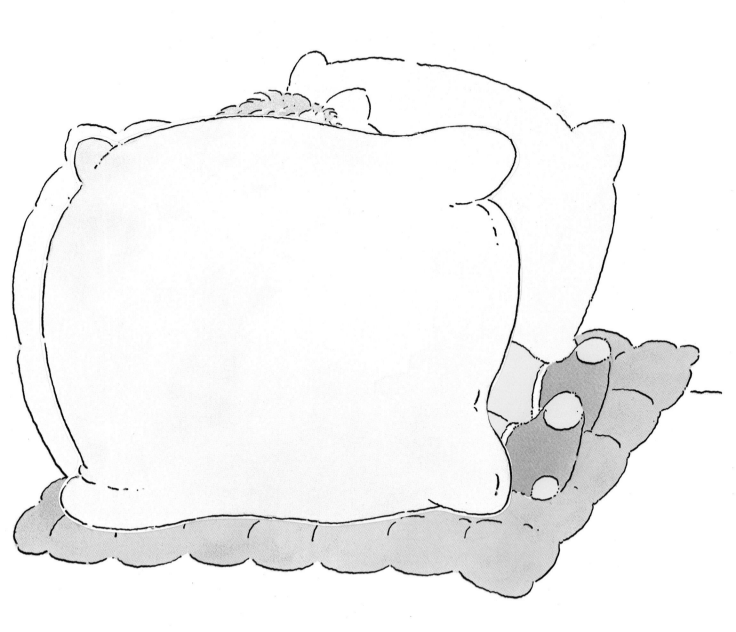

My first tooth

My first real dinner

My first bubble bath

My first pet

My first step

My first friend

My first word

My first party

Here's a picture of me!

VIKING KESTREL

Penguin Books Ltd, Harmondsworth, Middlesex, England
Viking Penguin Inc., 40 West 23rd Street, New York, New York 10010, U.S.A.
Penguin Books Australia Ltd, Ringwood, Victoria, Australia
Penguin Books Canada Ltd, 2801 John Street, Markham, Ontario, Canada L3R 1B4
Penguin Books (N.Z.) Ltd, 182-190 Wairau Road, Auckland 10, New Zealand

First published 1985

Copyright © Colin and Jacqui Hawkins, 1985

Printed in Great Britain